Joe's Bike Race

Also by Malachy Doyle

Carrot Thompson, Record Breaker
Just-the-Same Jamie

Joe's Bike Race

Malachy Doyle

Illustrated by
Michelle Conway

POOLBEG
FOR CHILDREN

Published 2001
by Poolbeg Press Ltd
123 Baldoyle Industrial Estate
Dublin 13, Ireland
E-mail: poolbeg@poolbeg.com
www.poolbeg.com

1 3 5 7 9 10 8 6 4 2

A catalogue record for this book is available from the British Library.

ISBN 1 84223 025 5

Cover design by Steven Hope
Illustrations by Michelle Conway
Typeset by Patricia Hope in Times 16/24
Printed by The Guernsey Press Ltd,
Vale, Guernsey, Channel Islands.

About this story

When I was eight I helped my Dad organise a big race, all round Whitehead. All my friends joined in. We went from my house, down Puck's Lane, up Cable Road, over King's Bridge, through the Garden Village, across the Raw Brae, past the Golf Club and back along the Belfast Road.

And guess who won? Me! (Well, me and Danny Haveron. Neither of us wanted to beat the other so we crossed the line together.)

For my Dad,

who got my picture in the paper.

"Dad! Dad!" said Joe, when he got back from school. "Miss Blackburn says there isn't enough money for us to go camping this year. Will you help me have a bike race?"

They did a poster on the computer.

JOE'S
BIG BIKE
RACE

**in aid of the
Churchtown School
Camping Fund
Barley Park
Sunday May 15
10.30 a.m.**

*£2 to ride or watch
£10 to the winner*

Next morning Joe showed his teacher, Miss Blackburn. She thought it was a great idea. So on Saturday Joe and his Dad went round town putting up posters in the shop windows.

3

Betsan from next door asked if she could join in.

"Of course," said Joe. "Anyone can."

"But it says it's a big bike race," said Betsan, "and I've only got a little bike."

Joe laughed. "That's OK," he said.

"Can Little Timmy come too?" asked
Betsan. "He's only got a three-wheeler."

"Of course he can," said Joe.

The sun was shining on the day of the
race.

"I'm going to win," said Joe to his
Grandad. "Just you wait!"

Dad pinned a sign to a tree:

Three-wheelers: one lap

Under eights: two laps

Under twelves: four laps

Everyone else: ask Joe.

Betsan and Little Timmy arrived.

"What's a lap?" asked Timmy.

"It means how many times you ride round the park. The bigger you are, the further you have to go," said Betsan.

"I'll win!" said Little Timmy.

"Oh no, you won't," said Betsan. "Because I'm much faster than you!"

Next came Pete. He had the twins with him, asleep in the back of his trailer.

"Six laps, Pete," said Joe. "And don't be too quick or you'll wake up Molly and Max."

Charlie Sprocket turned up with what looked like half a bike. It was a unicycle.

"Oh dear," said Joe's Dad, laughing. "What happened? Did you have a crash?"

"Just one lap, Charlie," said Joe. "I don't think you'll be very fast."

"Here come the real racers," said Mum.

Through the gates came three members of The Tigers, the local racing bike team.

"Twelve laps because you're speedy," said Joe.

"Hello, everyone. Isn't it a lovely day?"

"Hello, everyone. Isn't it a lovely day?"

It was Mr. and Mrs. Evans on their tandem, Daisy Daisy.

"Can they go twice as fast because there's two of them?" Joe whispered to his Dad.

"Oh, I don't think so," said Dad. "And they are quite old."

"Six laps," Joe told them.

Ringalingalingalingaling.

In came the strangest bike of all. It was a bit like Daisy Daisy but it was three times as long. On it were seven firemen.

"Morning, Joe," said the one at the front. "This is the Firebrigandem. Can we join you?"

"Of course you can," said Joe. He had a word with his Dad.

"Eight laps," he told them.

Miss Blackburn was collecting the money.

"How much have we got, Miss?" asked Joe.

"£40 already, Joe!"

"But it won't be enough to go camping, will it?" asked Joe, looking worried. "Not when we give a prize to the winner?"

"Oh, don't worry," said Miss Blackburn. "I've still a lot of people to ask."

A woman from the Evening News came to take a picture of everyone, and at 10.30 exactly, Grandad shouted, "GO!"

Everyone was off, with the Tigers racing and the Firebrigandem chasing, as if there really was a fire!

Then came Daisy Daisy, Dad and Mum, Pete and the twins and Betsan and Joe.

Last of all came Charlie Sprocket on the unicycle and Little Timmy on his three-wheeler.

They were just reaching the corner when the crowd started cheering. The Tigers had been right round already! They whizzed past poor Charlie so fast that he wobbled and fell off.

Suddenly Miss Blackburn burst out laughing. The firemen had turned on their hose and were spraying the crowd with water. Everyone was yelling and running away from the track.

Molly and Max, just behind, woke up and began to cry.

"Oh dear," said Pete. He cycled over to Jenny, who lifted them out. Grandad told Pete he could carry on with an empty trailer for now.

Then Grandad started telling Miss Blackburn about his schooldays.

"That building over there," he said, pointing to a large house just outside the gates, "was my very first school. Boys went in one door and girls in the other . . ."

At that moment the Tigers came racing towards him again. They saw Grandad pointing and, thinking he was showing them the way to go, zoomed straight out the gates and down the street!

They were soon back, looking cross. Grandad said he was sorry he'd mixed them up, and off they went.

When Pete stopped to pick up the twins again, Dad and the jolly firemen went past him.

Just behind, singing away to themselves, came Mr. and Mrs. Evans. The crowd joined in their song:

"Daisy, Daisy,

Give me your answer, do.

I'm half-crazy

All for the love of you . . ."

Mr. and Mrs. Evans rang their bells and waved.

The Tigers passed twice more before anyone else appeared. Then came Pete, the tandem and the Firebrigandem, all at the same time.

And behind were Joe and Betsan, pedalling hard. Miss Blackburn called them in for a drink so they wouldn't get too hot.

"But I can't stop, Miss!" said Joe, rushing past. "I have to win!"

Mum and Dad pulled in for a rest.

"Have you seen Charlie Sprocket and Little Timmy?" asked Miss Blackburn.

"Oh yes," said Mum. "Charlie's still going, and the last time I saw Timmy he was in the playground eating an ice cream!"

The racers were showing no sign of tiring and were zooming past for the ninth time when Grandad shouted, "Oi! You've left one behind!"

The front two stopped and the third one came running up, pushing his bike.

"I've got a flat tyre!" he cried.

Number one whipped the wheel off

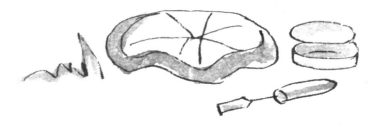

while number two ran to the car park. Dashing back with a new wheel, he handed it to number three who fixed it back on the bike before you could say "Tour de France."

Trailer, tandem, Firebrigandem.

Trailer, tandem, Firebrigandem.

Grandad waited till the Tigers had been past and then he held up a big sign for each of the riders:

Dad gasped, Mr. and Mrs. Evans sang, the firemen cheered and Pete waved.

The Tigers had to go round twice more before Grandad held up the sign for them.

Then a murmur went through the crowd.

"It's Charlie and Timmy!" someone called.

Sure enough, there they were, coming up to the finishing line ahead of everyone else.

Little Timmy looked worn out but Charlie was right beside him, "Come on," he said. "You can do it!"

Timmy's Mum ran over. "Come on, love. Keep going!"

The whole crowd took up the chant: "COME ON, TIMMY! COME ON, TIMMY!"

Suddenly Betsan and Joe appeared in the distance.

"I've got to win!" cried Joe, pedalling as hard as his poor tired legs would go.

Charlie and Timmy were nearly on the line, closely followed by Betsan and Joe. And then lots of other bikes appeared! It was Mum and Dad, Pete and the twins,

Daisy Daisy and the Firebrigandem, all racing furiously.

"Watch out!"

Everyone looked down the track and there, flashing out of the trees, were the Tigers.

"Come on, Joe!" shouted Grandad.

"Come on, Timmy!" called Timmy's Mum.

"Come on the Tigers!" yelled the rest of their team, who'd arrived just in time.

And would you believe it? All the bikes reached the finishing line at exactly the same time!

The crowd went wild. Timmy's Mum ran over and hugged him, and the twins woke up and yelled for more food.

Everyone was smiling, except Joe.

"What's the matter?" said Miss Blackburn. "It was a great race."

"I wanted to win," said Joe, sadly.

"You did!" said his teacher.

"Yes," said Joe, nodding, "but so did everyone else. If we have to give £10 to all the winners, there won't be any money left!"

"Ah," said Miss Blackburn.

"You see," said Joe, "if I won, I was going to let you keep the prize so that ALL the money was for camping."

So Miss Blackburn spoke to the riders and they all agreed that they'd had such a good time, they'd be quite happy if no one got a prize.

And then she made a speech.

"Thanks to Joe for having the race," she said, "and to everyone else for coming along. We've raised seventy-two pounds and we'll be able to go camping!"

Everyone cheered one last time, and Joe smiled happily.

THE END

Just-the-Same Jamie

by

Malachy Doyle

Jamie doesn't like change.
He likes everything to be just the same.
Including Aunt Alice.

But one morning Aunt Alice comes to visit
And she isn't the same at all.

She's wearing a shiny black leather suit
And she's riding a super-charged
motorbike!

And there's a leather suit and
A helmet for Jamie too . . .

Just-the-Same Jamie

by

Malachy Doyle

Available from Poolbeg,
the Irish for bestsellers

ISBN 1-84223-003-4

Carrot Thompson, Record Breaker

by
Malachy Doyle

Carrot Thompson was born to break records.
When she gets a Stop Watch and the
biggest book of Records for her birthday –
World Record Breakers look out!

Roller-Skate limbo dancing! Spitting a
watermelon seed! Tossing pancakes!

Carrot and her friend Marcus
don't know where to start!
So they start by hopping to school, clapping.
The one leg clapping world record
could soon be theirs . . .

Carrot Thompson, Record Breaker

by
Malachy Doyle

Available from Poolbeg,
the Irish for bestsellers

ISBN 1-85371-932-3

The Fox's Tale

by
Don Conroy

Redstart's Mum says he's too young to go outside the den at night.

But when he peeps out he sees the moon's children, the stars, in the sky.

"How come they can go out at night and I can't?" says Redstart

And so he decides to go and explore . . .

The Fox's Tail

by
Don Conroy

Available from Poolbeg,
the Irish for bestsellers

ISBN 1-84223-052-2

The Origami Bird

by
Lorraine Francis

The Origami Bird sits on the schoolroom windowsill.

He wants to fly, like the birds he sees outside. But he can't because he is made out of paper.

"I will fly!" he says.

"I'm a bird. I have wings. I'll fly high in the sky!"

Can his dream possibly come true?

The Origami Bird

by
Lorraine Francis

Available from Poolbeg,
the Irish for bestsellers

ISBN 1-84223-019-0

A Present From Egypt

by

Stephanie Baudet

A great big post-office van arrives at
Sam's house.

That means a parcel!
Maybe a present from Uncle Max?

It IS from Uncle Max
AND IT'S A CAMEL!

BUT WHAT WILL THEY DO WITH IT?

"Right now it can start on the lawn",
says Mum. "I've been meaning to mow
it for a week"

Sam's family are soon wondering how
they ever lived without a camel.

A Present From Egypt

by

Stephanie Baudet

Available from Poolbeg,
the Irish for bestsellers

ISBN 1-85371-960-9

Double Bubble Trouble

by

Stephanie Baudet

Gran has lost her glasses again!
"Four slices of jam and a pound of
carrots, please," she says peering
at her shopping list.

Sarah thinks it's all a giggle.

Until Gran uses the new bubble bath . . .

'SQUAWK!' Says Pip the Budgie,
hopping on his perch.
Is he trying to tell them something?

Double Bubble Trouble

by

Stephanie Baudet

Available from Poolbeg,
the Irish for bestsellers

ISBN 1-85371-977-3

LuLu's Tutu

by
Lorraine Francis

Lulu loves her new tutu.

It is as white as sugar and light
as candyfloss!

Tomorrow she will be the
Sugar Plum Fairy on a real stage.

But the tutu has other ideas . . .

When a gust of wind blows it off the
washing-line, it flaps into the air like a
bright white bird and flies off on
an adventure of it's own . . .

LuLu's Tutu
by
Lorraine Francis

**Available from Poolbeg,
the Irish for bestsellers**

ISBN 1-85371-951-X

THE END

good time, they'd be quite happy if no one got a prize.

And then she made a speech.

"Thanks to Joe for having the race," she said, "and to everyone else for coming along. We've raised seventy-two pounds and we'll be able to go camping!"

Everyone cheered one last time, and Joe smiled happily.